My Journey Through Life And Love

Leutisha Danielle Walker

ENTEGRITY
CHOICE PUBLISHING

Author's Note

I began writing in high school for assignments. I was struggling with a lot in high school, and I began to write one day about what I was going through. I learned that writing about what I was going through helped me feel better. It helped me to express my feelings and frustrations in a positive way. I became so use to writing in high school that I began to write for fun. I was always writing about something. In high school, I was focused on dating different boys, finding and keeping the right friends, making good grades in all my classes, and pleasing others. At times, it was stressful, so I wrote about those things.

In college, I faced a lot of challenges as well, which led me to continue writing. This was during the time that I was ready to get my degree, find someone to settle down with, and start our family. I wrote about everything I was going through because my frustrations were high. I noticed that things were going slower than what I wanted them to. I was ready to be done with college. I was ready to find my future husband. I was ready to have my own little family. Nothing was going my way, so I wrote about it. I learned that I was writing from my heart. When I write from my heart, words flow out.

I stopped writing for a while because I started to try to handle what was going on in a negative way. This led me to depression. It brought back feelings from my past, and tore me apart more. I began to feel like nobody cared about me. I felt like my life was falling apart, and that I couldn't go on anymore. Every way I turned, it was depressing. I turned to my friends at school, and didn't get anywhere. I turned to people at church, and felt that they only hated me. I felt that I didn't belong. I turned to God, and he restored my joy. I began writing again. I knew that as long as I had God, I was going to be alright. Things started getting better. My smile was back. I still faced a few challenges, but I held my head up high.

I became pregnant with my son, and faced a lot of challenges again. It seemed as if everything was falling apart all over again. My son's father and I couldn't get our acts together, so we kept breaking up and making up. I ended up tired of everything. I made up in my mind that I wasn't dealing with the same mess I dealt with already in my past. I had to be strong. I had to keep pushing on. I had to do what was best for my son and me. Some may wonder if I found my happiness. I found it in God. He blessed me with one of my greatest blessings thus far, which is my son. He keeps me pushing on.

Now, I continue to write because it makes me feel better by getting my frustrations out, and so I can share my story with someone that may be going through the same thing I went through. Whoever this book is for, I pray that you will read my story and be inspired to push on in life and achieve your goals.

Contents

PART THREE
My Years Now

PART ONE

My High School Years

Ups and Downs of Life

When everything goes wrong,
Why is it so easy to give up?

When friends turn their back on you,
Why is it so easy to never talk to them ever again?

When a relationship fails,
Why is it so easy to never trust again?

When things are turned all around and upside down,
Why is it so easy to want to die?

It's life.
It comes with its Ups and Downs,
We just have to be strong,
And keep moving on.

Life is not perfect,
Neither are we,
We were made this way,
So shall it be.

When things go wrong,
Look at the good things that are,
Not the bad things that were.

When friends leave your side,
Don't forget there are other ones that will always be there.

When relationships don't work,
Remember there are more fish in the sea.

When things are turned around and upside down,
Trust that the Lord will send you through.

Can't Let You Go

Everything and everybody is telling me to let you go,
I go to do it,
But then there's something stopping me.
I wonder to myself, "What could it be?"
Looks…love…maybe even personality…
Who knows?
I don't.
All I know is I can't let you go.

I find myself always thinking about you,
Always wondering what you are doing when I already know,
Wishing you were somewhere next to me,
Keeping me some company,
Carrying on our lives so happily,
Giving no care in the world to the stuff that goes on around us.

There's something about you that I'm holding on to,
I don't know if it was the fact that you had called me your boo,
Or if it is something else that you may do,
All I know is that I'm starting to fall in love with you.

We may argue,
We may fight,
Knowing always that we will be tight,
Whether as friends or lovers,
I guess that's all that matters,
As long as you're in my life,
Someway,
Somehow,
You'll always be there.

No matter where we go in life,
No matter how far away,
You will always be in my heart,

Cause you're here to stay,
Forever and always,
Because I can't let you go.

You're always on my mind,
Every minute and every hour of the day,
Dreaming about you in every kind of way,
Thinking about our future,
Hoping soon to be together,
Because…I can't let you go.

Change In A Day…But A New Beginning

It's amazing how a person can change in a day.
How everything can be fine at one moment, but then turn all
around the next.
How you can think everything is going good between y'all,
But then everything changes.

It's amazing how everything can change so fast,
When it was like yesterday when y'all were having fun.
How y'all would talk to each other every day,
And message each other all the time,
And put each other before work and anything else.
How you introduced them to the family and friends and vice versa.
How y'all could spend so much time together,
And have kodaks that would help remember the fun times.
It's all weird.

It's kind of sad, too, how people can just keep a happy face,
When deep down inside they are hurting…
They are crying…
They are feeling like no one truly cares about the way they are being
treated…
Just feeling empty…
Depressed…
Disappointed.

It's kind of hard to clean up a broken heart…
All the little pieces…
Getting smaller and smaller…
Hoping to be put back together…
To love…
To hold…
To cherish.
You may wonder when that can happen?
When can everything go back the same?

When will you be happy again?
Maybe soon,
Maybe later,
But maybe you have to let the past go,
As well as the pain.

It's going to be hard,
But you can do it.
Just think…
It's a new beginning.

Wishing You

As I am sitting here,
Thinking,
Thinking about you,
Wishing you were here,
Hoping and praying that you are okay,
I sit here and realize how my life would be without you.
Everything would change,
My life,
The world,
Everything you can possibly think of.
I would be heartbroken,
Torn into pieces,
Wishing you would come back.
Life…would it be able to go on without you?
The world…will it be able to?
Me…I would, but it may take me a few days…weeks…even months…
But I wouldn't want to have to be without you.
You know you have my heart,
And I have yours,
Forever your love will stay,
And so, will Mine, too.
You know I will always love you.
I just wanted you to know that I'm wishing you were here,
And I'll always love you.

Life Is Too Short

Life is too short to be worried about all your problems,
All the good ones,
And the bad ones to follow along.

Life is too short to have all this conflict in
the world that we have today.

Life is too short,
So you need to get ready because He's coming back.

What way,
What order,
In any form,
He's coming back because life is too short.

Be nice to your neighbor,
Be nice to your friends,
Be nice to the ones that are your enemies, too.

You never know when your last time may be,
So get ready,
Get set,
Because He's coming back,
Because…life is too short.

To My VT Friends: A Lost Tragedy

My buddies,
My pals,
My friends till the end,
I know you been through some things,
But I'm here to tell you,
Everything will be fine,
Just keep holding your head up.

These problems come just to make you strong,
Just hold on because it's just a test,
A test that you may have to keep going through,
Or maybe a test just for you to learn.

Learn from all the mistakes that y'all have seen,
And help it to guide you in the right way.

I know you guys are really hurting from the loss of your friends,
family,
And people you just knew,
But everything will be okay because God is watching over you.

So don't worry,
Mourn for a little,
But not for long,
They are in a better place,
And hope you will be in a better place soon too.
I love you guys,
So take care and be strong.

Someone Special

To that special someone,
That God has brought for me,
From up above,
I love you.

Thank you so much for being there for me,
Through the times I wasn't feeling good,
Through the times I just needed to talk.

We haven't known each other for a long time,
But I know that you are the one for me.

You're my baby,
You're my love,
You're everything I ever wanted.

Although I may not always say I love you,
I really do,
And you know that boo.

Our love is so true,
So don't take it for waste,
Because you could lose me and lose my heart,
And that would hurt you more than most.

So be good to me,
Treat me right,
And wonder to yourself,
What an amazing sight.

Remember Sweetheart

My sweetheart,
My love,
I love you oh so dearly.

Remember the day that we first met,
It was love at first sight.

Remember the night that you invited me over to your house,
That night I will never forget.

Remember that was our first long talk,
That good talk.

Remember when you made me smile,
Oops,
I forgot,
That's all the time.

Remember the day when you found out I liked you,
It was just like yesterday.

Remember the day you found out I loved you,
Yea,
And I still do.

You're my love,
My heart,
My big baby,
My honeybun,
My sugar in my Kool-Aid,
Everything you can possibly think of,
And not to forget,
My only sweetheart.

You Were Always There

You were always there when I needed you,
You are always there to watch everything I do.

You have been here for me since I was a baby,
And I know you will always be.

Thank you for loving me,
It means so much as you can see.

I know it's pretty hard to be a special mom,
But to let you know,
You are the bomb.

You are so honest,
So gentle,
So friendly,
So trusting,
So giving,
And so, sharing.

Thanks so much for showing your tender care,
It helps me to know you will always be there.

I just wanted you to know…

My arms are spread like wings of a dove,
My heart is with so much love.

For you're more precious than a pot of gold,
And my love for you is more than my heart can hold.

Momma, I truly love you.

How Wonderful You Are To Me

Oh how wonderful you are to me,
You're great,
You're amazing,
You're my joy that God has sent for me.

God sent you into this world just to make me happy,
And I'm truly glad you're here.

My life feels so complete now that I have your love,
And I thank Him from up above.

I really miss you right now,
But I know soon you will be home.

I know it gets lonely and boring over seas and working for the
Navy,
But think, soon you will be home,
Sitting and laying in my arms.

So just go on and finish up what you have to do there,
And rush home as soon as you can,
So we can finish what we began,
Until we reach the end.

I miss you oh so much, baby,
The hugs and kisses, too,
But you know you will always be my boo.

Think about those hugs,
So warm and comfortable,
Me in your arms.

Think about the kisses,
How it was so real,
And yet, just so wonderful, just like you.

You're everything I have been looking for in a guy,
You know how to make me happy,
You know how to make me smile and laugh,
I know you will never hurt me.

I really pray you will be mine forever,
And forever you will stay,
Because you should know by now,
How wonderful you are to me.

What Do I See?

What do I see?
Some people ask me,
I see people,
I see animals,
I see everything around me,
I see guys,
I see girls,
I see their attitudes, too,
I see guys loving girls,
And girls loving guys,
I see the way they look at each other,
The way they look at me.

I see the guy I like,
Yet he doesn't recognize me,
I see the eyes of the guy that I like,
Looking at me,
I see the way he looks at me,
And then whispers to his friends,
I see the way he smiles at me,
I see the love that is coming my way.
I see him standing right beside me,
And I think and imagine, is this really what I see?

I see what I need to see,
I see what I want to see,
I see everything that is happening to me,
I see the day passing by,
I see the guy I like after school,
And he sees me.

I see the guy freeze and smile at me,
I see my feet moving,
Walking his way,

I see a girl that could be his girlfriend,
I see myself falling away,
I see myself not getting my way,
I see the next day that same guy,
I see my heart being put back together,
I see life creating all over again,
I see this guy walking my way,
I see the butterflies in my stomach,
I see him looking at me,
I see him staring at me,
And then I see him ask me out.

I see myself dreaming,
But it's actually real life,
I see us dating,
I see us kissing,
I see that we have fallen in love,
I see forever.
I see my life getting better,
I see that I have felt something,
And I see that he has felt the same,
I see that we will now be together,
Forever,
I see life and love,
That's what I see.

SOLs

I hate them.
They suck.
I got told Monday,
I will have to take two more.
I have to take them over because I need them to graduate.
I have to graduate,
I'm not being stuck in high school no longer.
I am seventeen years old,
And next year I'll be eighteen.
I have to get ready to be by myself.
I have to learn how to be on my own in life,
I can't do that unless I take these boring SOLs.
I think I am ready,
BRING THEM ON!

So Much Stress

So much stress,
In this world today.
I am so stressed,
I don't know what to do.

So much stress,
I tell you,
I tell you again,
There's so much stress,
So let's begin.

I have SOLs next week,
They're a pain in the neck,
I feel like a big geek,
Because I feel like a total wreck.
I have Science,
Biology,
And Algebra,
Not to forget the other homework I have.

So much stress,
Building,
Building,
BUILDING,
On top of me,
Can't you see,
All the stress,
I try my best.
I don't think that's enough, I guess.
I have so much on my mind,
I feel like I am in a complete bind,
So much stress.

I sit here waiting impatiently,
Biting my nails terribly,
I can't stop it.
Little by little bit,
I begin to think.
I am under a lot of stress,
Too much for me.

I feel like all I can make is a "D."
I know I can do better,
That's what I'm here for.
Still thinking,
And thinking,
And thinking some more,
So much stress.

These SOLs are messing me up,
I wouldn't be stressed if it wasn't for them.
I'm going to study,
Study,
Study,
And study some more,
Till it's time for me to take the SOLs.
I won't stop,
I won't let them get to me,
I can do it if I keep my mind focused on it,
But too much stress.

I have the homework,
It has to be finished by Friday,
I have these tests in other subjects,
Like on Monday,
Spanish,
Spanish,
Spanish,
La Universidad.
Too much stress!
I have to stay focused,

But it's not working,
I have too much stress,
Like thinking about the upcoming stuff,
Thinking about my report card that has to be extremely good,
I'm going to be grounded if it's not,
My mom said so.
Thinking about that special someone,
Thinking about my godbaby that will be born in June,
But so much stress.

PART TWO

My College Years

A Forever Love From God

Look at what God has created for me,
A dream,
Maybe even a fantasy,
A guy that seemed so gifted,
So smart,
But yet so misunderstood.

He was reluctant with the problems in life,
The people,
The hard times,
And even love.

He was searching for love in all the wrong places,
He needed someone that would care for him,
And cherish him,
Someone that could inspire him.

Maybe he was in my dreams because he was meant for me,
He was made physical,
So I could see him,
Touch him,
Smell him,
Or even hear him.

In this dream,
I met him and he met me,
I knew this love would forever be.

Then someone's anger and frustration ended his life with an
assassination,
His death seemed to aggravate me,
Until I woke up in his arms,
Where I'll forever be.

Hurting

Sometimes life may bring its happy times,
But it can also bring some disappointing times.

Sometimes I sit here and wonder,
Why do some of these things happen?
I never really knew until one Sunday not too long ago.

I always thought it was because of the stupid things we did in life,
But my pastor told the church,
It's because it's just LIFE.

I still knew that my knowing why those things happened,
Still didn't answer for why I was hurting so bad.

I started thinking to myself,
To discover why I was hurting so bad.

It's because I deal with guys,
And the way they treated me.

I've been hurt OH so bad over the years,
But here recently is why it left me hurting and all so confused.

This guy, I thought, was my lover and friend,
I found out he really wasn't.

He was nice,
Flirty,
And just caught my attention.

One day we were talking,
He said he liked me and wanted to be mine forever,
And I felt the same about him,

But I F
E
L
L
for him so hard,
The things that happen after that just tore me apart.

Those crazy things that happened,
Made me feel like I just could not go on anymore.

I was hurting,
Torn into pieces,
Hating the fact I dated him and told my mom I wanted her to meet him,
BIG MISTAKE!

I started doubting everything and gave up on life,
Until this one guy wanted me to be his.

I felt like pieces of my life and body were being put back together again.
I felt like I could go on again,
But then I had a battle of my ex and this new guy.

I really loved my ex,
But he has hurt me before,
So I decided to be with the new one.

Now that I am with him,
I feel COMPLETE,
And SPECIAL,
And LOVED.

He treats me the way I want to be treated,
Loves me for me,
And does things for me that no guy has ever done for me,
And I love him.

Now all the hurting is gone,
And now finally I can go on.

An Empty Love

My life feels empty without you,
You were the reason it changed.
Before I met you, I was going nowhere,
But through a world of sin,
You made me want to better my life,
And make it right,
It was you that challenged me in having God first.

Our visions became the same,
Helping one another make it to Heaven.
You were always there for me when I needed you,
Through my trials and tribulations,
Always there to pray for me and with me.

I was always thankful for that,
But one day things changed for the worse,
I felt like we were drifting slowly apart,
What was happening to this man of God who I loved?
As we slowly pulled apart,
My heart slowly teared apart,
I can't go on this way!
God made you for me,
For this I know,
So where does our love go from here?

In Love

Am I in love or am I not,
Everything I ever wanted I found it in you.

Your smiles,
Your laughing with all that sense of humor.

I tell you the truth,
You truly make me happy.

It's just what I needed and wanted,
Someone to keep me feeling like I am somebody.

These special feelings I have for you,
Makes me feel like we were meant to be.

Ever since the day I first met you,
I knew we would talk once again.

I appreciate your friendliness,
Your kindness,
Your feelings of comfort,
I appreciate everything you have done for me.

I've always wondered how things would be without someone
cheating on me,
And I'm thinking you are the one that will be
the one who will change all of that.

I really do have feelings for you because…
I think I'm in love.

Could It Be Love

Is it true love or is it just my imagination?
Is it what I want or what I feel?
Is it me just dreaming or is it really happening?
Is it my wish that's in my heart or a trick my mind is just playing on
me?
Where do I go from here?
Is it somewhere near?

This trip down Love Street keeps me informed and upbeat.

I wish, I wish, I wish!

I wish a million things,
I wish more!

Why can't I tell what's love?

Love can be confusing,
Love can be amusing,
Love can be like the little birds chirping,
Love is peaceful,
Love is gentle.

Do I have time for love or do I not?

What could it be?
Could it be love?

I Have Found the Right One

I have been through so much,
But it was all a learning experience.

Some things I never wanted to happen,
But yet they happened,
But the good thing is,
It is all over now.

I have found the right one,
The one that treats me like no other.

He's different,
And I thank God for bringing him into my life.

It's time for me to let go,
And let go of the past.

It's time to look at my future,
And see what God has in store for me.

Yes, the past lingers around in my memories,
But the Lord lets me know that I have no worries.

About this right one I've found,
He sees things the way that I see them.

He tells me, "Yes, church is more important than anything,"
Which is something the others didn't realize.

He is so Sweet,
Honest,
Loving,
Caring,
Pretty much everything I ever wanted.
He's so protective,
Which reminds me of my dad.

He's someone that will listen to anything I say,
That reminds me of my mommy.

Some fail to realize that,
But the things he tells me,
And how he treats me,
Proves that he is not like the others,
And that I have finally found the right one.

What Must I Do

I don't understand how I can be with someone else,
And have these feelings for you, too,
But yet, that night I was thinking about you,
Trying to fall asleep.

But yet, I couldn't close my eyes,
All because of you,
Constantly thinking about you,
Wondering what must I do,
Wishing that we were spending time together at that moment,
Just a little longer.

Wishing that we had one more night up here together,
But yet, I knew that tomorrow we would have to
go our separate ways,
I stared out the window at all the lights,
Not wanting to rest my head on my pillow because it
would soon be over,
I tried to convince myself that it was wrong to want to
be with you,
But yet, that's hard to do,
When you're mad at your boo,
It's also hard because every time I see you,
I try to look like you get on my nerves,
But then you just end up making me smile…
Something's not right!

This is all wrong!
I can't do this!
I prayed for happiness,
And I received it,
But now I'm all confused again,
Because I have all that I need with some wants,
Where do I go on from here?

I don't know,
But Lord, please help me.

I Love the Way You

I love the way you make me smile,
I love the way you make me laugh,
I love the way you look at me,
I love the way you talk to me,
I love the way you act,
I love the way you do everything.

You Are

You are the one that keeps me happy.
You are the one that keeps me going.
You are the one that I want to spend the rest of my life with.
You are my heart,
You are my sunshine,
You are the one that brightens my day,
You are the one that I'm falling in love with more and more each
and every day.

I'm Not Supposed To

I'm not supposed to love you.
I'm not supposed to care.
I'm not supposed to live my life wishing you were there.
I'm not supposed to wonder where you are or what you do,
I'm sorry,
I can't help myself because I'm in love with you.
I only get jealous because I love you,
And I don't want nobody else to have you.

My Love Doctor

My heart has stopped beating emotionally,
Someone please come take care of me,
Place the pieces gently back together with your love and your care,
Show me what doctor I should have and not the one that I had.
Give me a doctor, who can put these pieces back together with no pain,
Without putting me to sleep,
Knowing that everything will be alright.

I Thought I Knew You

I thought I knew you,
Evidently, I didn't.
Look at the person you have turned into,
Looked into your eyes and I thought you were the one,
But evidently you were just a playa trying to get you some.
How could you break my heart and tear it into two?
After the way you made me smile,
Laugh,
And see you differently than any other.

I have made mistakes before,
But dating you was my biggest mistake of them all,
But I learn from my mistakes,
And I will learn from this one, too,
Not to date jerks just like you.

There are other fish in the sea,
So don't think I need you,
I have lived life before I knew you,
And I can still live after knowing you.

Life still goes on,
You think I care,
But really I don't,
You can try everything,
Never will I care.

Missing Everything About You

I'm missing everything about you,
The way you talk,
The way you look at me,
Your touch,
Your kisses,
But most of all your smile.
Sometimes I find myself lying in bed,
Thinking about you,
Possibly driving down the road thinking of you,
How you used to make me happy,
And how you would make me smile.
But more than anything,
The times we spent together,
But now that we are over,
I'm missing everything about you more and more.

My Love

I don't know what it is about you,
But I can't let you go.
You have stolen my heart,
And when I thought you had given it back,
I turned around and realized you still had it.

You bring out my true self that everyone loves,
The way I used to be before I started getting hurt,
Before then I was always happy and smiling,
Everyone loved that side of me,
Until I began to get hurt by these players out here these days.

They hurt me,
Tortured me,
Abused me until they couldn't abuse me no more,
Leaving me in pain and tears,
Enough to make my own river,
But then I met you.

At first, we were just friends,
Then you became something more to me,
My soulmate,
My best friend,
My love who I wanted to spend eternity with,
You brought joy to my life again.

When people saw me, I had a new look about myself,
My smile had become brighter than the sun itself.
You turned my world upside down,
It was you that made life worth living,
Even the times when you made me mad,
You continued to keep a smile on my face,
When at first, I felt like knocking you out,
You make it so hard to want to turn against you,

And leave you.
I'm still strong.
If I had one choice of who to spend the rest of my life with,
It would be you.
You have treated me like no other,
And for that I am grateful,
You make my past and my sorrows disappear,
I want to continue having you in my life.

You keep happiness in my life when sadness tries to creep in,
I know we have had some rough times here lately,
But I am willing to fix those problems as long as you are willing to
do the same.
When I first met you,
Who would have thought you would be the one to hold my heart.
I love you!

Time Will Tell

I trusted you with my heart,
And look what happened,
You broke it anyways,
Causing me pain,
My heart to be broken,
Into pieces.

Don't you think I have suffered enough?

I thought you were different,
When really you were the same,
You made it seem at first like you really loved me,
And cared about me,
But as time progressed,
I started to see the true you,
Nothing different than any other.

I gave you my love,
And what did you do,
Took it and played a game.

Now that you are back,
Trying to continue being in my life,
I debate whether or not you are meant to be in it.

I think about all the good times we have had,
But also the bad,
You still may be the one for me,
But time will tell.

I Will Wait for You

My heart slowly tore apart…
Slowly…
Wanting to decay and rot away because it couldn't go any farther…
WAIT!!!

Just when I felt the need to give up,
God brought you into my life.

Is this just for one season or until eternity?
I know it was a reason,
I feel that God has brought you into my life
because you're the one for me.

He has seen me struggling and on the edge of falling off the cliff of
life,
And decided to give me you,
You are the best thing that has happened to me!

You are not perfect,
But you are perfect for me,
You're everything I've ever wanted in a man.

All of these boys before you just don't know how to treat a girl right,
They lied,
They cheated,
Did me wrong.

I notice that you are way different,
You brighten up my world,
You always make me smile and laugh,
Even when you're nowhere around.

I've never found someone so perfect as you,
This is why I will wait for you.

Lost In a World of Sin Without You

I almost let you go out of my life,
But something told me to keep trusting in you,
So I did.

I came to know,
That that was the best decision ever.
Since I allowed you to stay in my life,
My life has changed for the better.

The things I used to do,
I don't want to do anymore,
The things I use to say,
I don't say no more.

It's all because of you, Lord,
And the change you have made in me.
When I think about all you have done for me,
And where you have brought me from,
When I couldn't see no way out,
And I almost gave up on everything,
I lift my hands to say, "Thank you, Lord for saving me."

If it wasn't for your grace and your mercy,
I don't know where I would be,
So I give you the praise that you deserve,
Because without you…
I am lost in this world of sin.

Forever Everlasting

I just want to hold you in my arms again,
And tell you how much I love you,
How much I miss you.
It's been too long,
I've been lost without you,
Ever since the day we went our separate ways.
Our love is still holding on,
Through all the hurt and the pain,
Never dying,
But forever everlasting,
You have my heart,
And I have yours.
Forever it will stay.
I love you.

Will We Ever Be Again

I don't understand how I'm supposed to let you go,
When I have fallen in love with you,
Can't you see what joy you have brought into my life?
Why would I want to just give that all up?

You lighten up my world,
With your smile,
Your eyes,
Your hugs,
And your kisses.
What happened to me being the Ying to your Yang,
The chocolate frosting to your cake…delicious,
You mean so much to me,
Words cannot explain.

God knew the desires of your heart,
And the desires of my heart,
So he decided to bring me you,
Bring you me.
Baby, I know I can be hard to deal with at times,
But baby, if you would please give me the chance,
You will understand that I love you so much.

The thoughts of losing you,
I cannot bear it at all,
My heart is broken,
Like a shattered glass,
Broken into small little pieces,
With every piece needing and wanting you.
Every moment without you,
Tears me apart more and more,
I can't understand why I felt this way about you,
So soon, so fast, so suddenly, I love you,
What more can I say?

There's this deep feeling inside of me,
That tells me that you still love me,
I feel that we were brought together for a reason,
And that we fell in love so easily because it was meant to be,
I just wish that you could see,
That my heart still beats for you.

Letting Go: Be Happy, Be Free

As I look out at the dazzling water,
I begin to think about how God created things to be.

As I look around,
I see people who are smiling, laughing,
Enjoying the nature that surrounds them.

There's a group of people here,
That have disabilities,
But they are enjoying life,
The way people should.

I sit here, thinking about them,
And I start letting go of my hurt,
My pain and the things that are stopping me from
living life the way God intended me to.

Sometimes we take life for granted,
Sometimes we let the trials and tribulations in our life bring us
DOWN.
But as I look around and see how happy and free the people are
around me,
I feel the joy,
Love,
And care,
That God wants me to share.

Peace…it's what I needed,
As I journey on to my next destination.
And it's time to say goodbye to the people around me and the
beautiful sparkling water,
The spirit of being free and being happy,

Lingers on in my heart,
Letting me know everything's going to be ok.

Before I leave,
I let the waves of the water,
Take all my hurt,
All my pain,
Everything in my past,
Slowly away…
Drifting away…
To let all my sorrows go.

I am happy now,
I am free now,
Thank you, Lord,
For saving me.

PART THREE

My Years Now

I Wonder If This Is True

I wonder if it's love or is it lust,
It can't be love because I don't really know you,
But I want it to be.

I wonder why I can't get you off my mind,
Every time I stop to think,
I notice I'm thinking about you,
Wishing you were here,
Somewhere near.

It's really bad when I'm asleep and I'm still thinking about you,
In my dreams…
In my thoughts…
In my heart…

You say I will be yours one day,
And I want you to be mine,
I've known you for a while now,
But in reality, I don't know you at all.

I wanna get to know you,
I wanna see what it is about you that I'm so attracted to,
Why it is that you keep leaving me feeling so good inside.

I know I'm with someone else now,
And you are coming out from being with someone, too,
But it's you I want to be with,
It's you my heart is longing for,
It's you I want to spend my life with.

But I constantly wonder…
Is this true?

I Love You

I love you,
You mean the world to me,
More than you will ever know,
My love for you is like no other,
And I'm thankful to have a man like you.

I know I'm not the easiest to get along with,
But do know that I love you.

If I never got the chance to say it to you,
Just know I love you from the bottom of my heart.

You keep me happy,
You keep me laughing and smiling,
Without you I would still be going through depression,
Feeling empty inside,
Not caring about all of my transgressions.

You're my heart,
You're my soul,
You're my love that will last forever,
You're my stars in the sky,
You're my dream of all dreams.

When you came back into my life,
At first I didn't notice you,
But as time went by,
I saw the way you looked at me, and smiled,
I smiled back when really, I was melting inside,
Wanting you all to myself.

That day you caught my attention in so many ways,
I remember it like it was yesterday,
A time to reunite our love,
Our love that didn't have the chance years ago,

Only because we never gave it a chance,
I wish we would have,
But the opportunity is back again.

This time I want it to be,
I want to be yours this time,
In all ways, not just one.

I want to show you that I love and care about you,
But I need you to give me the chance,
Be patient with me,
Be patient with us,
We can't rush things,
For if we do,
We may destroy what we can have.

I know sometimes it seems like I don't care about you,
But I truly do,
If I could, I would give you anything you wanted,
I would even give you the world.

When you're happy,
I'm happy,
When you're sad,
I'm sad,
When you feel like no one cares,
Remember that I care and I always will.

I wish I had the courage to tell you by mouth,
How much I love you and care about you,
But every time I get the urge to tell you,
I let the negative come and change my mind,

I apologize,
But this is the way you will have to deal with me telling you for
now,
At least until I feel comfortable enough to tell you face to face.

I love you to the moon and back,
From sunrise to sunset,
'Til death do us part,
You will forever be in my heart,
I love you.

62

My Past Is My Past

I guess my love for you will never matter,
Despite my past,
I knew I wanted you in my future.

When we stopped talking years ago,
I didn't know that years later I would fall in love with you.
All I want now is you,
Nothing else matters in life,
I was asked what I wanted for my birthday and Christmas,
And all I could think about was wanting you.
I want you,
I need you,
I love you,
The thought of losing you tears me apart.

I don't want to imagine my life without you,
I don't want you to not be a part of my life,
Having you in my life has made life more enjoyable,
My past is my past,
It can't be changed.

Mistakes have been made,
And yet I'm ashamed,
I've learned from those mistakes,
They've made me stronger,
They've made me better,
Made me into the person I was meant to be.

If God can forgive me,
You should be able to forgive me, too,
I know I should have told you from the beginning,
But I was scared that you wouldn't want to be with me.

Now that you've found out,
I'm scared that I've lost you.
Yes, I have a past,
But everybody has a past.

Don't criticize me for my past,
'Cause everyone has made mistakes,
I wanted to leave my past behind,
But it has come to bite me in the butt.
Although it has surfaced again,
I will not let it destroy my future,
It's just up to you if you want to be in it.

It's Going To Be Alright

My heart breaks again,
I feel empty inside,
Fooled once again,
One day I will learn.

This is too much for one to bear,
But, Lord, I know that You know how much I can handle.
Make me stronger,
Make me wiser,
Help me to be careful who I trust.

I go from being happy to being sad to being happy all over again,
It's called depression,
I need to get out of it,
And stay out.

It's the same cycle,
What's wrong with me?
Nothing, you say,
I'm made in Your image,
So why do I still get treated this way?

Do they fail to know You?
Please help me,
I need You,
I can't make it without You,
You've been there for me all along,
And I still need You to depend on.

Instead of laying here crying,
I will turn everything over to You,
For I know that You will make everything alright.

I Feel

I feel hurt,
I feel broken,
I feel lost,
I feel confused,
I feel pain in my heart,
I feel the tightness it brings,
I feel tears falling down my face,
I feel like I cannot go on,
I feel betrayed,
I feel used,
I feel like you never loved me at all,
I feel like you were never mine,
I feel that we don't have a future,
I feel that I need to move on,
I feel that life is drifting slowly by,
I feel unhappy,
I feel that I will never get what it is that I want in life,
I feel that everyone around me is happy,
I feel like my heart has been crushed all over again,
I feel numb to the pain,
I feel like I need to cry but I have no tears left,
I feel hopeless,
I feel the same as I did before,
I feel like my life has come to an end,
I feel…
Nothing…

Come Back Baby

I just want you back,
I miss you more than words can tell,
The love we had we still share,
It has never left,
And it never will.

We've made mistakes,
But nothing can break the bond that's there,
I want to go back to the days we were happy together,
Laughed together,
Spent time together,
When you would hold me,
As I fell asleep in your arms,
When you would look at me,
And easily make me smile,
When nothing else mattered,
As long as I had you,
And you had me.

Together forever,
That's where I want to be,
A life without you is meaningless,
Pointless,
You complete me.

I've never been as happy as I was when you were a part of my life,
Even the days when you made me mad.
Now that you're not in it,
My heart breaks over and over and over again,
'Cause all it wants is you,
It wants you back,
It needs you back.

My knight in shining armor,
To me anyways,
That's all that matters,
That I love you,
And I always will,
So please...come back.

68

Finding Me

I feel like I've lost a part of me,
My heart feels like someone has stabbed it,
Broken it,
Put it all back together,
To break it all over once again,
This time in little pieces that's too hard to be glued back together,
Leaving me feeling like a part of me is missing.
What is this that I am searching for?
Is it love?
Is it time?
Is it happiness?
Or could it be who I am?

Where is my encouragement,
My motivation,
My strength to go on?
It's all missing,
Can it be found?
Calling all search teams,
I need to find me,
Search high,
Search low,
Search left,
Search right,
To the mountains,
To the valleys,
Down below,
We're looking for me!
Beautiful,
Kind,
Loving,
Filled with joy,
Patient,

Intelligent,
One of a kind,
Me needs to be found,
In a quick,
In a hurry,
Time is running out,
Me is slowly dying,
Beep...beep...beep...
I've seem to have lost a part of me,
But will it ever be found?
....Beeeeeeeeep....

I Trust You

I'm going to trust you, Lord,
Because I know what You are capable of doing,
Just look around at all the things You have done,
It helps me to hold on,
To be still,
To let You work things out,
I'm not sure what You have planned for me,
But whatever it is,
Don't do it without me,
Time will tell,
That You can do all things,
That there is no other,
Who made the life on Earth possible,
Who is constantly working daily for us, His children,
I will trust you, Lord,
That you have better in store for me.
I will keep my head up,
I will keep pressing on,
I will keep smiling through all of my pain,
Because I know that you will never leave me,
Nor forsake me.
For I know that I am more than a conqueror,
And this too shall pass,
Because...I trust You.

Butterflies

How do you tell someone that you like them?
It seems like the words want to flow out your mouth,
But there's something stopping them,
It's how you feel,
It's what's in your heart,
But there's something inside stopping you,
Is it fear?
Is it your past?
Is it what others will think of you?
Or could it be butterflies,
I don't know,
But I do know that I like you.

When I see you,
I begin to smile,
When I see you,
My heart races,
When I see you,
I pray to God you will be mine one day,
When I see you,
The butterflies start to flutter,
Oh, how I feel so nervous inside,
Lord, please help me,
You know the desires of my heart,
And it is you that can make all things possible,
I put my trust in you,
I walk by faith and not by sight,
For I know you have chosen him for me.

Butterflies, please go away,
Fly away into the breeze that blows,
Be free,
Let go.

I'm Just Tired

I'm tired of all the lies,
I'm tired of not feeling appreciated,
Not loved,
I'm tired of being used,
I'm tired of the sometimey people in my life,
That call themselves my friends,
My lovers,
My none like no other,
I'm tired of trying to please you when in reality I need to please
myself,
I'm tired of not doing what's best for me,
I'm tired of others making all the decisions,
I'm tired of going in circles,
I'm tired of feeling alone,
I'm tired of the games,
I'm tired of the bull,
I'm tired of hiding and covering up my hurt,
Pretending everything is ok when really, it's not,
I'm tired of shedding all my tears,
I'm tired of being mistreated,
I'm tired of living in depression,
I'm tired of trying to be strong,
When really, inside, I feel weak but know I'm not,
I'm tired of going through,
I'm tired of all the negative thoughts,
I'm tired of asking God "Why me?"
Only to already know that it's just a test and that I'm still blessed,
I'm tired of feeling shame,
I'm tired of my restless nights,
I'm tired of the world doing the judging,
When really it should be God,
I'm tired of falling apart and having to pick up the pieces,

I'm tired of feeling empty inside,
I'm tired of losing my mind,
I'm tired of feeling like I did something wrong,
I'm tired of not feeling worthy,
I'm tired of feeling like I'm just a hit it and quit it,
I'm tired of being led on,
I'm tired of pushing you to do better in life,
I'm tired of having to baby you,
When I already have a baby on the way,
I'm tired of dealing with a momma's boy,
I'm tired of stressing about how things will be when the baby gets
here,
I'm tired of doing stuff to make me feel better,
I'm tired of feeling like a failure,
I'm just tired of being tired.

Time to Grow Up

I'm tired of all this hurt,
All this pain,
Begging you to care,
It's driving me insane,
Time to move on,
Time to find happiness,
My joy,
My peace,
My love again,
Don't you think my heart has been crushed,
Stomped on,
And kicked to the curve enough,
It stops here,
This game you are playing,
Leave it to the kiddies,
For that's what they're used to,
Grow up,
Be a man,
Let God use you,
And show you,
Which direction you should go,
Because it's time to grow up.

You Know, I'm A Strong Black Woman

You know I've been hurt,
Lied to,
Talked about,
Used and abused,
But yet I still stand.

You know my heart has been broken into two,
Crushed,
Put back together to be broken again,
Yet I'm still stronger than ever.

You know they say you will never make it in life,
You will never achieve your dreams,
Give up now,
Because you're nothing but a failure.

You know I've been criticized for being the color I am,
Who I am,
But yet I still hold on,
Holding on to hope,
Hoping for a change,
That change is near.

You know I've been put down for being a woman,
Being told I can't do this or that because I am one,
That I can never do what a man can do.

You know I still hold my head up high,
With everything I'm faced with in life,
Though I'm the subject of their tongues,
I still know I'm better than what's being said.

You know God made me,
He was the creator,
I've been through so much,

But it was the Almighty that ordered my steps,
It was the King of Kings that kept me pushing on,
Alpha and Omega,
The beginning and the end,
Who created my beginning and my end,
He who made me whole again.

I stand because of him,
I push on because of the strength He gave me,
I keep being myself because I know I'm made in His image,
This is why I'm A Strong Black Woman.

Being Strong

As I lay here and think about everything,
My thoughts,
My plans,
Life itself,
How I have to be strong on days that I don't want to be,
For me,
My son,
My loved ones.

I think about everything I've been through in life,
Wondering why I had to go through it,
Wondering why I can't have that "perfect" life,
Where I'm happily married,
Married with children of course,
Being one big happy family.

You know,
I tell you,
I'm strong,
I may cry at night,
Vent to my friends,
Want to give up,
Thinking life can't go on,
But deep inside,
I'm still strong,

Still fighting the fight,
Still holding on,
Having faith that he will never leave me alone,
I trust him,
To guide me,
To carry me,
To be my shoulder when I need one to cry on.

The Lord brought me here for a reason,
So I put on the full armor of God,
I stand up strong,
With the belt of truth,
The breastplate of righteousness,
My feet fitted with the readiness that comes from the gospel of
peace,
The shield of faith,
The helmet of salvation,
The sword of the spirit,
And continue to pray in the spirit.

I have no choice but to be strong,
To stay strong,
Even Jesus wept,
So why can't I,
I just have to remember,
That I'm more than a conqueror,
And that it was Jesus that has brought me this far.

The Kind of Man I Want

I want a man that will love me for me,
The good,
The bad,
Flaws and all,
That will love me unconditionally,
Someone who can show me how much they really care,
One who compliments me every time he sees me,
Makes me smile and laugh,
But also there when I need someone to lean on.

A person who listens,
But gives advice, too,
Corrects me when I'm wrong,
One who stands strong,
As a leader,
A father,
A true man,
Someone who is only committed to me,
Not playing games with my heart.

One who will be there for my son,
To show him how to be a man,
Teach him how to treat a woman,
To demonstrate the right way to live life,
A man who can think for himself,
Do for himself,
Someone who will always be there,
For better or worse,
For richer or poorer,
In sickness and in health,
Until death do us part.

One I don't have to push,
To do better,

Be a better person,
Someone who challenges me to do better and be better.

One who just wants to make me happy,
Someone who notices the little things about me,
Little things in life,
A man that will trust me,
Be honest with me,
Hold me,
Cherish me,
That's the kind of man I want.

How Much I Love You

You ask me how much do I love you?
I love you more than infinity plus one,
From the heavens to the earth,
All over the land and the sea,
I love you more than sweet tea.

You ask me how much do I love you?
I love you more than you will ever know,
From January to December,
All the days of the year,
I love you more than you kissing on my ear.

You ask me how much do I love you?
I love you more than words can say,
From the beginning to the end,
All over again,
I love you more than when we first began.

You ask me how much do I love you?
I love you more than to the moon and back,
From sunrise to sunset,
All around the world and more,
I love you more than I did before.

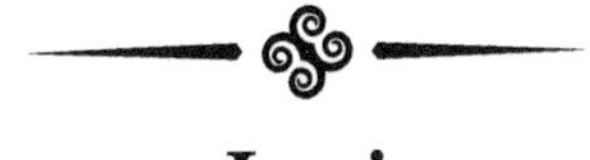

Levi

I remember the day you were born,
I held you in my arms,
An even seven pounds,
I loved you from then on out.
When I looked into your beautiful brown eyes,
My heart melted,
I was thankful to have you,
I was so glad you were finally here,
I looked at my mom and my stepmom and smiled all over my face,
I couldn't believe you were here,
I couldn't believe I had a child of my own,
Levi, you make my life so amazing,
You make it worth living,
I can't imagine my life without you,
Now that you have a part in it,
You may cry,
You may laugh,
You may drive me crazy,
But at the end of the day I still love you,
And I'll always love you,
No matter what,
When you're mad at me,
When you're sad about something I did,
Or when you're just happy,
You're my baby,
My love,
My blessing.

I Want Someone to Love Me

I want someone to love me,
Truly love me,
Love me for who I am,
Someone who will look beyond my past,
Look at our future,
Someone who can trust me,
One who won't believe negative things that's being said about me,
I want someone to love me, who will always be there,
One who will listen and show he cares,
Someone who won't let me do everything on my own,
I want someone to love me, who can be my backbone,
My motivation,
One who will take care of me when I'm sick,
Someone who wants the best for me,
I want someone to love me,
Through the thick and the thin,
From the beginning to the end,
Someone who will never let go,
I want someone to love me.

I Know Where My Heart Is

I know where my heart is,
For it is somewhere near,
Somewhere close by,
Not too far away.

I know where my heart is,
I can still feel it,
It still beats,
It still loves.

I know where my heart is,
It's miles away,
Kept in a special place,
That I can call mine.

I know where my heart is,
For it is somewhere safe,
Keeping warm,
Away from all harm.

I know where my heart is,
It's with a man I love,
He holds my heart,
And I hold his.

I know where my heart is,
Where it belongs,
With you,
Where it will forever stay.

P.O. Box 453

Powder Springs, Georgia 30127

www.entegritypublishing.com

info@entegritypublishing.com

770.727.6517

www.ingramcontent.com/pod-product-compliance
Lightning Source LLC
Chambersburg PA
CBHW071011120726
47910CB00004B/1478